CANADA

North Dakota

Minnesota

South Dakota

Wisconsin

Michigan

New York

Massachusetts

Rhode Island

Connecticut

Iowa

Pennsylvania

Nebraska

Illinois

Ohio

New Jersey

Indiana

West Virginia

Delaware

Maryland

Kansas

Missouri

Kentucky

Virginia

Washington, D.C.

North Carolina

Oklahoma

Arkansas

Tennessee

South Carolina

Mississippi

Alabama

Georgia

Texas

Louisiana

Florida

D1414693

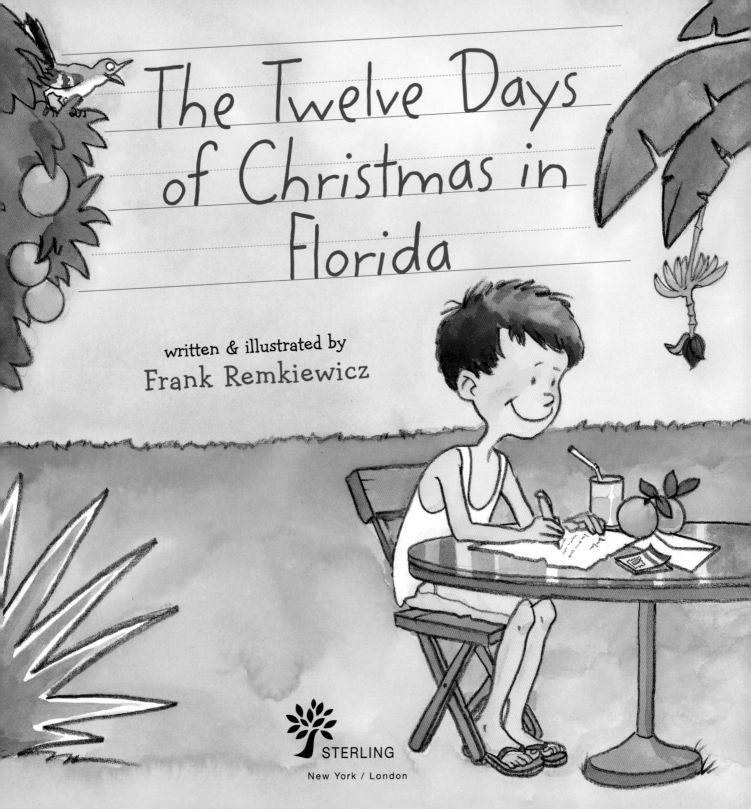

# The Twelve Days of Christmas in Florida

written & illustrated by
Frank Remkiewicz

STERLING

New York / London

Dear Luann,

Guess what?! Guess what?! You are coming here for Christmas vacation! We all chipped in, even Uncle Millard, then Mom went online, and here it is: your plane ticket to Florida! It's a window seat, so you can look down at the blue water, sandy beaches, and backyard swimming pools. Our pool is the one with the banana tree, the orange tree, and the water-basketball net. When you get here, we can drink freshly squeezed OJ while we shoot hoops!

Does your post office have a big truck? If not, they'd better get one soon, 'cause some super-size special deliveries are heading your way!

Twelve days to go. I can't wait!

Your cousin,
Travis

Dear Luann,

Can you imagine sitting under a palm tree on a warm sandy beach in the middle of December, listening to the squawks of seagulls? Well, all you have to imagine is the beach, 'cause here is your very own seagull in a sabal palm—our state tree! One of my favorite snacks is called swamp cabbage, made from the juicy center of the sabal palm mixed with a sauce that's sweet and sour and spicy all at the same time. Boiled peanuts are another tasty Florida snack. Uncle Millard makes them in his slow cooker with a secret recipe that he's going to sell for thousands of dollars so he can buy a new trailer or maybe a houseboat!

I hope you like the seagull. I almost sent you our state bird (the mockingbird) instead, but it's famous for copying all kinds of bird songs and even the sounds of other animals! I thought that might drive you (and your cat) a little crazy.

Bye for now,
Travis

On the first day of Christmas,
my cousin sent to me . . .

a seagull in a
sabal palm tree.

Dear Luann,

Did you know that FIVE different kinds of sea turtles swim in Florida's waters? The loggerhead and leatherback turtles both lay their eggs on our beaches. You probably won't see many sea turtles while you're visiting, but during the summer, there are about 50,000 of them here!!

Yesterday while we were fishing, we saw a huge sea turtle in the water. Its shell was kind of a brownish greenish reddish color. A turtle coming up for air is probably going back down to a reef to eat fish, and I guess he was, because pretty soon we caught enough keepers to fill up our ice chest.

There were lots of flying fish out that day, too. They are awesome! They could fly across our whole backyard without even touching the grass! When we got home, we had a big fish fry of grouper, snapper, and grunts. I caught all the grunts. (Don't laugh—a grunt is a kind of fish!)

You'll never guess what you're getting for the second day of Christmas. Keep them in a warm, safe place and bring them with you when you come!

Your cousin,
Travis

On the second day of Christmas,
my cousin sent to me . . .

2 turtle eggs

and a seagull in a sabal palm tree.

Dear Luann,

Today I had to give my dog a bath. Speed Bump was all muddy from chasing a squirrel that was carrying off one of our oranges in his teeth! The squirrel got away.

Cows like oranges, too. You should never let them into a grove because they'll eat all the fruit they can reach! There are a lot of cows here—did you know that Florida is the largest cattle-grazing state east of the Mississippi?

Old-time Florida cowboys were called cracker cowmen. All they needed was a horse, a dog, and a big long whip to crack. It was tough, dangerous work to catch cows that wandered off into the palmetto scrub and swamps. (Don't forget, the swamps are full of alligators, snakes, and mosquitoes!)

Speed Bump just loves swamps. I think he is part cow dog, because look what he found for you yesterday! Surprise!

See you,
Travis

On the third day of Christmas,
my cousin sent to me . . .

3 swamp cows

2 turtle eggs,
and a seagull in a sabal palm tree.

Dear Luann,

Guess what I'm making for my history project about the early settlers? Here's a hint: "Don't let the bedbugs bite." Give up? I'm making a pillow stuffed with Spanish moss, just like the settlers did. Only they didn't have bug spray, and luckily I do. (Often little bugs live in the moss and they are biters.) The Spanish weren't really interested in moss. They were looking for gold, spices, and the Fountain of Youth, but didn't find any of that stuff in Florida. They did leave behind a neat old fort in a city called St. Augustine, which they founded in 1565, making it the oldest city in the U.S.! The fort looks out over the Atlantic Ocean and has cannons for fighting off enemy ships or pirates. Some of the cannons still work . . . BOOM!

When the Spanish explorers left Florida, they found LOTS of gold in Mexico and Central America. They loaded up their ships with treasure, hoping to sail back to Spain with it. But getting through the dangerous Florida Straits wasn't easy. With sandbars, pirates, and hurricanes to deal with, it's no wonder that lots of ships sank to the bottom of the straits. Hey, let's go treasure hunting while you're here!

Nine days!
Travis

# On the fourth day of Christmas, my cousin sent to me . . .

4 Spanish ships

3 swamp cows, 2 turtle eggs,
and a seagull in a sabal palm tree.

Dear Luann,

Well, I got a B- on my early settlers pillow. Miss Leon said I would have gotten an A if I'd used a plain pillowcase instead of the one from Disney World.

In happier news, Granny Annie donated a Key lime pie for my school bake sale. Do you like pie? Do you like limes? If you do, you will LOVE Granny's Key lime pie. It has a graham cracker crust and creamy yellow filling, topped off with whipped cream and a swirl of real lime. Maybe you're wondering if she bakes keys into a pie. Not! A Key lime is a kind of small lime that grows in the Florida Keys. YUM!

Granny has a whole cookbook of just citrus recipes for oranges, lemons, grapefruit, and limes. Once she told me that citrus peels can even be made into cattle feed! You might think that citrus fruits are Florida's only big crop, but they're not. We also grow a whole lot of sugarcane—more than any other state! I'll ask Dad to take us to Lake Okeechobee (Okeechobee is a Seminole Indian word that means "big water"). All around the lake you'll see miles and miles of sugarcane fields. Yum again. Enjoy your pies!

Sweet dreams,
Travis

On the fifth day of Christmas,
my cousin sent to me . . .

5 Key lime pies

4 Spanish ships, 3 swamp cows, 2 turtle eggs,
and a seagull in a sabal palm tree.

Dear Luann,

Do you like Gatorade? Well, guess what? It was invented at the University of Florida for the football team to drink! Of course, they're called the Gators.

We saw lots of alligators in Myakka River State Park. We were canoeing, so it was a little scary. Alligators are supposed to be lazy and sleepy during the daytime, but I saw some that definitely were not sleeping. Feeding them isn't allowed because they might start thinking that people and food go together. No way!

A ranger told us that gator jaws can crunch right through a turtle's shell. That is serious snack time! Years ago, tourists were able to send little gators home as souvenirs and gifts. Some escaped or were abandoned and were found years later in the sewer systems of big cities! Sending baby gators to people isn't allowed now. Too bad, because, personally, I still think gators are a great gift idea. They could be very entertaining.

Your generous cousin,
Travis

# On the sixth day of Christmas, my cousin sent to me . . .

# 6 gators grinning

5 Key lime pies, 4 Spanish ships, 3 swamp cows, 2 turtle eggs, and a seagull in a sabal palm tree.

Dear Luann,

Did you know that you can call NASA and reserve a spot at the Kennedy Space Center on Merritt Island to watch a space shuttle lift off? How neat is that? I wish there were a shuttle launch scheduled during your visit. (I've seen one launch live and have videos of others. My favorite part is when the booster rockets fall off!) Since there isn't a shuttle launch, I've planned something else. I think you'll like it.

Daytona International Speedway is a short drive up the coast from the Space Center. Do you think it would be cool to be a race-car driver? I do. We can practice at the Pirate's Cove go-kart track if you want. It's right near my house. I have an extra helmet that will fit you. Get your camera ready and look out your window, 'cause your next gift is a <u>blast!</u>

Signing off,
Travis

On the seventh day of Christmas,
my cousin gave to me . . .

7 shuttles launching

6 gators grinning, 5 Key lime pies,
4 Spanish ships, 3 swamp cows, 2 turtle eggs,
and a seagull in a sabal palm tree.

Dear Luann,

We just went on a boat trip to Key West. What a neat place! Even though its name is Key <u>West</u>, it's actually way down on the tip of Florida and is as far <u>south</u> as you can get in the United States! It's one of a whole chain of about 1,700 islands that make up the Florida Keys. Granny says that Key lime pie is the official dessert of Key West.

Our boat left from Fort Myers, where we were touring the winter homes of Henry Ford and Thomas Edison. They were not only super-famous inventors, they were also neighbors!

Anyway, on the boat ride we saw lots of dolphins—wild dolphins! They swam and jumped through the air and could circle our boat in a flash. Wait till you see them spy hopping! That's a move that gets them upright on their tails so they can scope out the area.

The dolphin is our state saltwater mammal, so I thought you should get to know a few before you arrive.

Are you counting the days?
Travis

On the eighth day of Christmas,
my cousin sent to me . . .

8 dolphins dancing

7 shuttles launching, 6 gators grinning,
5 Key lime pies, 4 Spanish ships, 3 swamp cows, 2 turtle eggs,
and a seagull in a sabal palm tree.

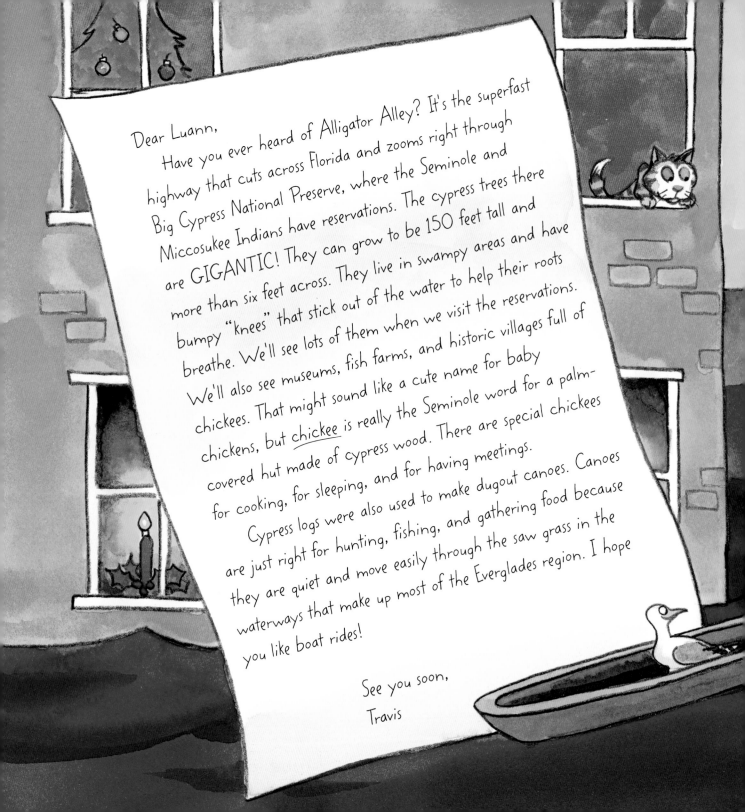

Dear Luann,

Have you ever heard of Alligator Alley? It's the superfast highway that cuts across Florida and zooms right through Big Cypress National Preserve, where the Seminole and Miccosukee Indians have reservations. The cypress trees there are GIGANTIC! They can grow to be 150 feet tall and more than six feet across. They live in swampy areas and have bumpy "knees" that stick out of the water to help their roots breathe. We'll see lots of them when we visit the reservations. We'll also see museums, fish farms, and historic villages full of chickees. That might sound like a cute name for baby chickens, but <u>chickee</u> is really the Seminole word for a palm-covered hut made of cypress wood. There are special chickees for cooking, for sleeping, and for having meetings. Cypress logs were also used to make dugout canoes. Canoes are just right for hunting, fishing, and gathering food because they are quiet and move easily through the saw grass in the waterways that make up most of the Everglades region. I hope you like boat rides!

See you soon,
Travis

# On the ninth day of Christmas,
# my cousin sent to me . . .

9 dugouts drifting

8 dolphins dancing, 7 shuttles launching, 6 gators grinning,
5 Key lime pies, 4 Spanish ships, 3 swamp cows, 2 turtle eggs,
and a seagull in a sabal palm tree.

Dear Luann,

What is tall, pink, and eats with its head upside-down? Give up? It's a flamingo! Our class saw lots of them snacking like that on our field trip to Flamingo Gardens. Miss Leon told us that flamingo babies are white when they hatch but turn pinkish from eating plankton and brine shrimp. They skim the water with their heads upside-down. A built-in strainer in the flamingo's beak separates the food from the water.

Uncle Millard has some flamingos—three of them—right by his hammock in the front yard. They are plastic, but I'm sending you some that are much better. If you don't have any brine shrimp around, just feed them lots of carrots and beets to help them keep their color nice and rosy.

So long,
Travis

On the tenth day of Christmas,
my cousin sent to me . . .

10 flamingos flapping

9 dugouts drifting, 8 dolphins dancing,
7 shuttles launching, 6 gators grinning, 5 Key lime pies,
4 Spanish ships, 3 swamp cows, 2 turtle eggs,
and a seagull in a sabal palm tree.

Dear Luann,

I told Granny Annie you wouldn't mind if she dropped in for a visit. She's in your area helping some of her "snowbird" friends pack up to move down here for the rest of the winter. They all love to play golf and go bird-watching. I think some of the birds they see here are the same ones that were in their yards up north before they flew south. These grannies migrate south, too. That's why we call them snowbirds.

Don't be surprised if they practice their golf games right in your living room while they show you pictures of their grandchildren. (Just say the kids are adorable and that you think they look smart!) Granny Annie will probably show you photos of her orchids, too. She has a whole room in her house just for them! A nice purple one is already decorating your bedroom here.

Two more days . . . yow!
Travis

P.S. Did you know that Florida has more golf courses than any other state? There are more than 1,250 of them here!

On the eleventh day of Christmas,
my cousin sent to me . . .

11 grannies golfing

10 flamingos flapping, 9 dugouts drifting, 8 dolphins dancing,
7 shuttles launching, 6 gators grinning, 5 Key lime pies,
4 Spanish ships, 3 swamp cows, 2 turtle eggs,
and a seagull in a sabal palm tree.

Dear Luann,

ONE DAY TO GO! Are you all packed? I am making a LUANN sign to hold up at the airport so you can find Uncle Millard and me in the crowd. Maybe people will think I'm a limo driver. That would be cool.

We drove past a "Panther Crossing" sign yesterday but didn't see any Florida panthers. (You are REALLY lucky that some wanted to visit you!) The panther is our state mammal, and it's an endangered species. Lots of people are working hard to preserve the panthers' habitats and keep them safe.

The manatee is our state marine mammal, and it's endangered, too. There are manatee zones along the Intracoastal Waterway where we drive our boat sometimes. We have to slow way down to idle speed in those places so the manatees will not get hurt.

I gave my early settlers pillow to Speed Bump. He moved it into the Florida room where you will be sleeping, so now you'll have a watchdog and an orchid for roommates. Mom says once you get sand in your shoes, you just keep coming back to Florida. I say, GREAT! We've got the sand, if you've got the shoes!

Your cousin,
Travis

On the twelfth day of Christmas,
my cousin sent to me . . .

12 panthers purring

11 grannies golfing, 10 flamingos flapping, 9 dugouts drifting,
8 dolphins dancing, 7 shuttles launching, 6 gators grinning, 5 Key lime pies,
4 Spanish ships, 3 swamp cows, 2 turtle eggs,
and a seagull in a sabal palm tree.

# Florida: The Sunshine State

**Capital:** Tallahassee • **State abbreviation:** FL • **Largest city:** Jacksonville
**State bird:** the mockingbird • **State flower:** the orange blossom • **State tree:** the sabal palm
(A.K.A. the sabal palmetto or cabbage palm) • **State animal:** the Florida panther
**State mammal:** the manatee • **State reptile:** the alligator • **State butterfly:** the zebra longwing
**State motto:** "In God We Trust" • **State song:** "Suwanee River"

**Some Famous Floridians:**

**Julian Edwin "Cannonball" Adderley** (1928–1975), born in Tampa, was a music teacher and jazz alto saxophonist in the 1950s and 1960s, known for playing with such jazz greats as Miles Davis.

**Jacqueline "Jackie" Cochran** (1906?–1980), born in west Florida, was a pioneer American aviator. She is known as one of the most gifted race pilots of her generation.

**Marjory Stoneman Douglas** (1890–1998) lived in Miami for many years. A journalist and environmentalist, she is best known for her 1947 book, *The Everglades: River of Grass*. This book inspired thousands of Floridians to combat overdevelopment in order to save the unusual environment of south Florida.

**Juan Ponce de León** (1460–1521) was a Spanish conquistador who traveled with Christopher Columbus on his second voyage to the New World and remained on Hispaniola (now the Dominican Republic). In 1513, he sailed north from Hispaniola in search of the Fountain of Youth. It is said that León gave Florida its name, *La Florida*, meaning "flowery," likely because he landed during Easter, known in Spanish as *Pascua Florida*.

**Marjorie Kinnan Rawlings** (1896–1953) was a famous author who lived for much of her life on an orange grove near Hawthorne. Her best-known novel, *The Yearling*, is about a boy who adopts an orphaned fawn. The book won a Pulitzer Prize for fiction in 1939 and was later made into a popular movie.

**Janet Reno** (1938–), was born in Miami and grew up in a house built by her parents at the edge of the Everglades. She was the first female Attorney General of the United States (1993–2001).

STERLING and the distinctive Sterling logo are
registered trademarks of Sterling Publishing Co,. Inc

**Library of Congress Cataloging-in-Publication Data**

Remkiewicz, Frank.
The twelve days of Christmas in Florida / by Frank Remkiewicz.
p. cm.
Summary: On each of the twelve days before her Christmas visit, Luann's cousin Travis sends her a letter describing the history, geography,
animals, and interesting sites of Florida. Uses the cumulative pattern of the traditional carol to present amusing state trivia at the end of each letter.
ISBN 978-1-4027-3817-3
1. Florida--Juvenile fiction. [1. Florida--Fiction. 2. Letters--Fiction. 3. Cousins--Fiction. 4. Christmas--Fiction.] I. Title.
PZ7.R2835Tw 2008
[E]--dc22
2007043648
6  8  10  9  7
05/17
Published by Sterling Publishing Co., Inc.
387 Park Avenue South, New York, NY 10016
Text and illustrations copyright © 2008 by Frank Remkiewicz
The original illustrations for this book were created in watercolor
Designed by Scott Piehl
Distributed in Canada by Sterling Publishing
c/o Canadian Manda Group, 165 Dufferin Street
Toronto, Ontario, Canada M6K 3H6
Distributed in the United Kingdom by GMC Distribution Services
Castle Place, 166 High Street, Lewes, East Sussex, England BN7 1XU
Distributed in Australia by Capricorn Link (Australia) Pty. Ltd.
P.O. Box 704, Windsor, NSW 2756, Australia

*Printed in China*
*All rights reserved*

Sterling ISBN 978-1-4027-3817-3

For information about custom editions, special sales, premium and
corporate purchases, please contact Sterling Special Sales
Department at 800-805-5489 or specialsales@sterlingpublishing.com.

Gatorade® is a registered trademark of The Quaker Oats Company, a unit of PepsiCo Beverages & Foods, Chicago, IL 60604-9003.

Walt Disney World® is a registered trademark of Disney, Lake Buena Vista, FL 32830-1000.

For Kelly and Lexi,
staffers extraordinaire.